There's a Witch
IN YOUR BOOK

Written by TOM FLETCHER

Illustrated by GREG ABBOTT

PUFFIN

For Buzz, Buddy and Max – T.F.

For Rose – G.A.

PUFFIN BOOKS

UK | USA | Canada | Ireland | Australia | India | New Zealand | South Africa

Puffin Books is part of the Penguin Random House group of companies whose
addresses can be found at global.penguinrandomhouse.com.

www.penguin.co.uk
www.puffin.co.uk
www.ladybird.co.uk

First published 2020

004

Copyright © Tom Fletcher, 2020
Illustrated by Greg Abbott

The moral right of the author has been asserted

Printed in China

A CIP catalogue record for this book is available from the British Library

ISBN: 978–0–241–35739–2

All correspondence to:
Puffin Books, Penguin Random House Children's
One Embassy Gardens, 8 Viaduct Gardens
London SW11 7BW

EEEK!
There's a WITCH in your book!

What a **mess** she's making!

Wipe the mess away and turn the page.

Well done! You cleaned up the mess!

But – **UH-OH** – now Witch looks cross.
I don't think she likes us un-muddling her mess . . .

WATCH OUT...

She's about to turn you into a toad!
Quickly, **hold up your hand** to block the spell . . .

Phew!
You caught the magic in your hand.

What a cheeky witch! Let's teach her a lesson
and turn *her* into something instead.

Use your finger as a **magic wand**
and say these words:

Magic this, magic that,
Turn this witch into a cat!

The spell worked!
You turned the witch into a stinky little cat!

But look – she has **fleas**!
And they're hopping all over your book.

Use your **magic wand finger**
and say this spell:

Magic silly, magic funny,
Turn each flea into a . . . bunny!

OH NO! We didn't think that through.
Now your book is **full of bunnies!**

OK, I know just the spell to get rid of bunnies.
Finger wands ready:

Magic far, magic near,
Make the bunnies disappear!

WHOOPS!

Those bunnies are *see-through* now,
but they're STILL IN YOUR BOOK!

Now they're bubble bunnies!

Hmm – try poking all the bubbles
with your magic wand finger . . . .

Aaargh!

Those bubbles were full of slime!

Now your book is *even messier*
than it was before.

Oh dear! This has all gone horribly wrong.
If only we knew someone
who could put everything right . . .

Oh, yes! **WITCH**, of course!
Do you think she might be more helpful this time?

Let's try turning that stinky little cat
back into a witch.

Finger wands up!

Magic scratch, magic itch,
Turn the cat into a witch!

Great – Witch is back!

And I think she has
a spell to help us . . .

Will this clean up the slime?

WIZWHACKEROO!!

Ooooh!
 Her spell made a hole in your book.

And she has a plan . . .

Done! Your book is all tidy.
Thank you, Witch.

Done! Your book is all tidy.
Thank you, Witch.

Use your hand to help Witch swoosh all the slime

ait a minute . . .

ou swooshed the slime through the hole,

ust mean that now your room is messy!

Take a peek through the hole at your room . . . .

PHEW! I can't see any slime,
but I do think your room could be a bit ti[d]
don't you?

(And when you tidy up, please – **NO MAGIC SPELLS!**)

Now you have such a tidy book,
I think it's time for a spooky sleepover.

Shall we do **ONE MORE SPELL?**

Yes!

Use your **magic wand finger** to make some spooky sleepover guests appear!

Magic snoozy, magic dozy,
Call some friends and let's get cosy!

It worked!

Have a fun sleepover, little spooks . . .

(Try not to make *too* much mess!)